A Sticker Story™

Bears in the Basement

Mary Blocksma and Sherry Long

Illustrated by Jane Dyer

Developed by The Hampton-Brown Company, Inc.

HPBooks

About Your Sticker Story™ Book

Here is a book children can read and have fun with again and again. Children participate in the story by adding stickers to pictures as the adventure unfolds. To begin, tear out the page of stickers near the front of the book. As children read the book, they will find flip-ups at the bottom of different pages. These flip-ups tell the child which sticker to select from the sticker page and where to place it in the picture. After reading the story, stickers can be removed from pictures and placed on the storage page near the front of the book. Stickers can be removed from that page to provide hours of fun each time the book is read.

Your Sticker Story™ is educational, too! Applying stickers gives children practice in comprehension as they match pictures to text. The vocabulary used in the story reinforces important words children are learning to read in school. Over 80% of the words in the story are commonly taught by the end of first grade.

Published by HPBooks
P.O. Box 5367
Tucson, AZ 85703
(602) 888-2150

For HPBooks:
Publishers: Bill and Helen Fisher
Executive Editor: Rick Bailey
Editorial Director: Randy Summerlin
Art Director: Don Burton

For The Hampton-Brown Company, Inc.:
Project Editor: Elisabeth Meyer Wechsler
Designer: John Edeen

ISBN: 0-89586-203-4

4.6199512953

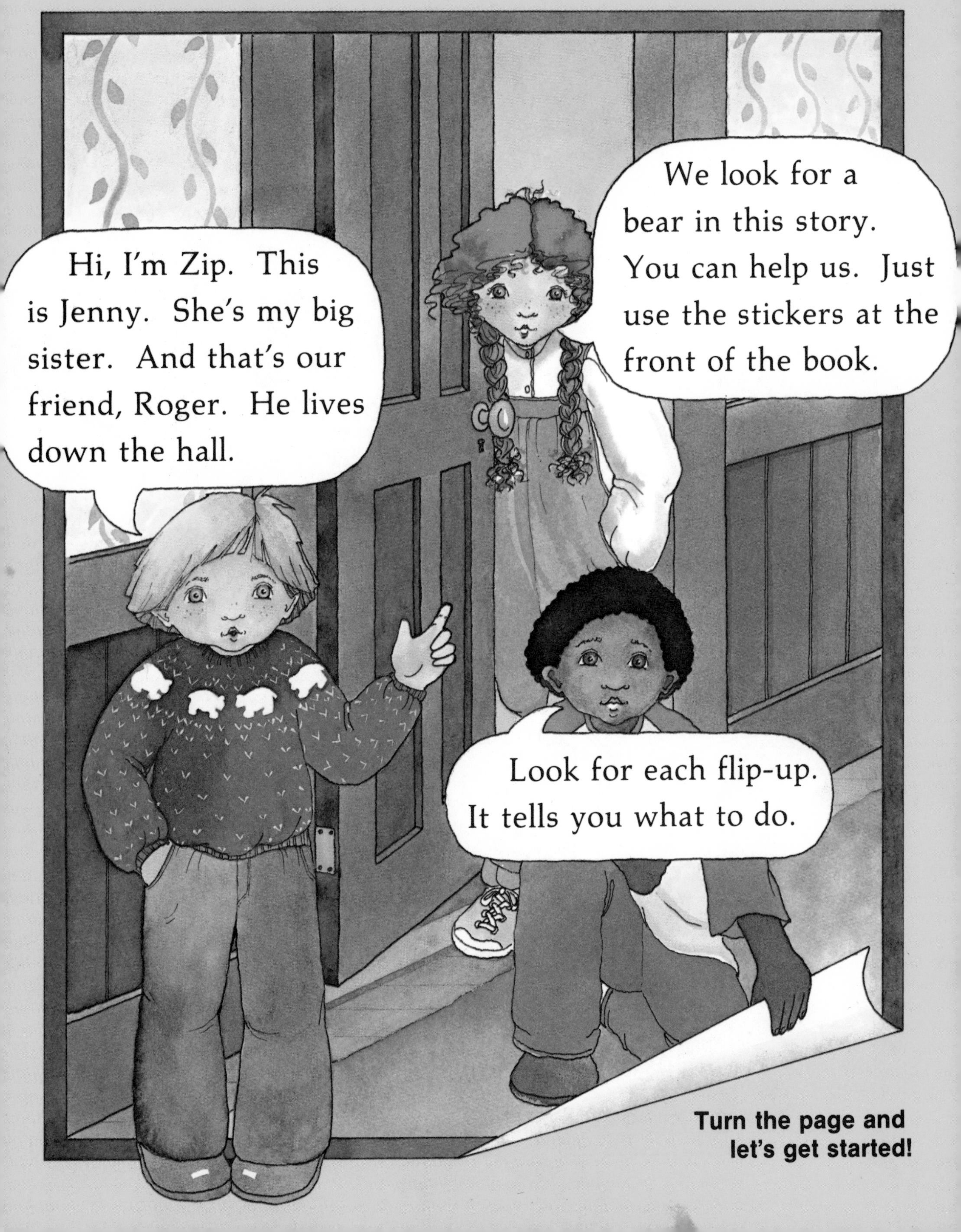

Turn the page and let's get started!

Dad was packing Zip's bag.
Roger and Jenny were helping, too.

"There," said Jenny. "Now
you're ready to go to Grandma's."

"I can't," said Zip. "I can't
find my teddy bear. I can't go
ANYWHERE without Henry!"

"I washed Henry with your
other things," said Dad. "I must
have left him in the basement."

"I have to get Henry,"
said Zip. "But I don't like the
basement. It's dark down there."
"Jenny and I will go with
you," said Roger. "Get your
coat. It's cold down there, too."

Zip, Roger, and Jenny ran to the elevator and got on. Jenny pushed the B button for basement.

"Oh, look!" said Zip. "Now the B button looks like a bear. So, Henry must be down in the basement!"

Use a sticker to turn the B button into a bear.

The elevator went down and down. It got colder and colder.

"Brrrr," said Jenny. "It feels as cold as a cave."

The elevator doors opened.

"It IS a cave!" cried Zip. "Do you think Henry is here?"

"He must be," said Roger. "Bears like caves."

Jenny and Zip started down the tunnel.

"Wait!" said Roger. "It's too dark. You can't go down there without lights and a rope."

"But I don't see any," said Zip. "What will we do?"

Use
stickers to help the
kids out. Give Roger a rope.
Give Zip a flashlight. Give Jenny a head lamp.

"Look," said Jenny. "Now we can see. Come on!" Off she went into the tunnel.

Roger went in after her. He was glad to have the long rope.

Zip went in last. He turned his flashlight on the wall. "Better watch out for these big bugs," he said.

The children went farther into the tunnel.

"I hear bats," said Jenny.

"It's just those hangers," said Roger.

Zip turned his flashlight up slowly. "No, Jenny's right," he cried. "They ARE bats. Look how big they are!"

Use a sticker to turn the hangers into bats.

The bats began to fly.

"Let's get going," said Jenny.

Zip asked, "What about that big, black hole?"

"We'll have to go around it," said Roger.

"Not me!" cried Zip.

"Just hold on to the rope, Zip," said Roger.

Slowly, the children walked around the hole.

"Don't look down," said Jenny.

"I can't," said Zip. "My eyes are shut."

The children made it past
the big hole.

"Where do we go now?" asked
Roger.

"I don't know," said Jenny.
"Let's keep looking."

Zip pointed to something on
the wall. "What's that?" he asked.

"It's just a sign," said Roger.

"No, it's a cave painting,"
said Jenny. "It will help us
find our way."

Use a
sticker to turn
the sign into a cave painting.

"The cave painting says to go that way," said Roger.

"It also says that bears are there," said Zip.

"Let's go see," said Jenny. "Follow me."

The children started to go into the room. They saw a sock in a big puddle of water. Zip stepped in the puddle.

"Yuck!" said Zip. "My feet are wet!"

"You're standing in a cave pool," said Roger. "Watch out for cave fish. They don't have eyes!"

"No eyes?" cried Zip. "Oh, no!"

"Here comes a fish now!" said Jenny.

Use a sticker to turn the sock into a cave fish.

Zip jumped out of the puddle. The children looked around. Along the cave walls they saw some big, round things.

"What are those?" asked Jenny.

"They're dryers," said Roger.
"No. They look like beds where bears sleep," said Zip.
"Maybe Henry is in that one," said Jenny. "Listen to that funny noise."

Use a sticker to turn the dryer into Henry's bed.

Jenny looked inside.
Slowly, she put her hand in.

Then she pulled her hand out.
A bear came out, too.

"It's Henry!" yelled Zip.

Just then, the children heard
a noise. They saw something
at the far door.

"What's that?" asked Roger.

"It's a REAL bear!" cried Jenny.

Use a
sticker to put
a big bear at the door.

"Help!" yelled Zip. "I have to get Henry out of here."

"I have to get ME out of here," said Jenny.

"Run!" cried Roger.

"There's that fish again," said Zip.

"Jump over it, Zip," said Jenny. "It's just a sock."

Use a sticker to turn the cave fish back into a sock.

Zip jumped over the sock. Then he ran so fast that he got to the big hole first.

"What if I drop Henry in the hole?" he cried. "I'll never see him again."

"I'll hold Henry," said Roger. "You hold the rope."

"Hurry," said Jenny. "The bear is coming after us!"

Next the children ran under the bats.

"What if they fly at us?" asked Zip.

"Use your flashlight, Zip," said Roger.

Zip pointed his flashlight at the bats.

"There," said Jenny. "Now they look like hangers."

Use a
sticker to turn
the bats back into hangers.

Zip, Roger, and Jenny raced to the elevator. The bear was right behind them. Zip pushed the button for their floor. The doors shut just in time.

The children got off at their
floor. They raced from the elevator.
"Let's hide in Zip's room,"
said Jenny.
"Why?" asked Roger. "Bears can't
work elevators."
"You never know," said Zip.

The children ran into Zip's room and hid behind his bed. Just then, something opened the door to the room.

"Oh, no!" cried Jenny. "It's the bear!"

"Bears CAN work elevators," said Roger.

The bear looked around the room. "Where are you, kids?" he asked. "I went to the basement to find you. But you all ran away."

"That's not a bear," said Zip. "That's DAD!"

Use a
sticker to turn
the big bear back into Dad.

Zip ran over and gave Dad a
big hug.

"Did you find your bear, Zip?"
asked Dad.

"We found TWO bears," said Zip.

"They were in a cave," said Roger.
"One was Henry."

"And the other gives the best
bear hugs in the world," said Zip.

"Is that so?" said Dad. And
he hugged all three children at once.
He even hugged Henry.